For Logan, Quinn & Tommy,
my heart & soul & my very own
little manic monkeys.

—R.S.

To all the girls I've loved before.
Especially my Mom.

—S.C.

Pappy particularly prefers
positively perfect pizza.

Written by Sean Covel
Illustrated by Rebecca Swift
Graphic Design by Laurel Antonmarchi and Marisa Randles

ISBN 978-1-7327501-5-9

Hoarding Porter, LLC
PO Box 173
Deadwood, SD 57732
www.porterthehoarder.com

Printed in China

From the Producer of **NAPOLEON DYNAMITE**

PORTER

written by Sean Covel

illustrated by Rebecca Swift

THE HOARDER

AND PAPPY'S PERFECT PIZZA PARTY

created by Rebecca Swift & David Cenaffra

HOARDING PORTER, LLC
DEADWOOD, SD

This pretty much looks like your refrigerator, doesn't it?

pickled pig's feet

purple packages of mozzarella cheese

Salty salmon eggs

Slices of Spicy Pepperoni

tub of tangy tomato sauce

Crispy crunchy chocolate-covered grasshoppers

Sizzling platter of liver and onions

moldy muenster cheese

ANCHOVIES 4 LIFE! ?

roll of puffy pizza dough

This is Porter.

She's a hoarder.

This is how you tell.

Aisles and piles of grocery goods,

so much to see and smell.

What you need to know about Porter is, when she goes grocery shopping, she always tries to take home the whole store.

Porter's Pappy's Pizza Party is tonight,
and he has requested his all-time favorite pizza
topping from Gunther's Grotesque Grocery
to make a Pepperoni Pizza.

Last time Porter made a pizza, it weighed 212 pounds and included toppings such as cheddar cheese, an ant farm and old tires. That atrocity must not happen again.

If Porter picks only the proper toppings for Pappy's Perfect Pizza, she gets to take home her very favorite snack...

ANCHOVIES!

Sometimes Porter gets a little distracted
when trying to complete her tasks. Can you
help her focus on finding the right toppings
for Pappy's Pepperoni Pizza?

Ready?

Let's GO!

Help Porter find ten pickled pig's feet.
Can you find all ten?

Should she buy the 10 pickled pig's feet?

NO!

Help Porter find nine purple
packages of mozzarella cheese.
Can you find all nine?

Should she buy the 9 purple packages of mozzarella cheese?

YES!

Help Porter find eight small jars of salty salmon eggs. Can you find all eight?

Should she buy the 8 small jars of salty salmon eggs?

Help Porter find seven slices of spicy pepperoni. Can you find all seven?

Should she buy the 7 slices of spicy pepperoni?

YES!!

Help Porter find six sizzling platters
of steaming liver and onion.
Can you find all six?

Should she buy the 6 sizzling platters of steaming liver and onion?

NO!!

Help Porter find five full tubs of tangy tomato sauce. Can you find all five?

Should she buy the 5 full tubs of tangy tomato sauce?

Help Porter find four crispy, crunchy
chocolate-covered grasshoppers.
Can you find all four?

Should she buy the 4 crispy, crunchy chocolate-covered grasshoppers?

Help Porter find three round
rolls of puffy pizza dough.
Can you find all three?

Should she buy the 3 round rolls of puffy pizza dough?

YES!

Help Porter find two massive mounds
of moldy Muenster cheese.
Can you find them?

Should she buy the 2 massive mounds of moldy Muenster cheese?

Porter picked the perfect toppings for
Pappy's Pepperoni Pizza.

Can you help her find her single
favorite snack?

The
End.

ABOUT THE AUTHOR

SEAN COVEL is a film and television producer who grew up in a blip of a town in the Black Hills of South Dakota. He has made over a dozen movies including the iconic independent film, *Napoleon Dynamite*.

Together, Sean's movies have played lots of places, won a bunch of awards and — most importantly — got nerds prom dates across the globe. He very much wishes that would've been the case when he was in high school.

Additionally, Sean is a children's book author (as you probably divined since you are, in fact, reading this at the back of a children's book). He's written the crazy children's book series, *Porter the Hoarder* (which you knew) as well as *Muffle Your Snuffle* (a book about sneezing without being a booger canon) and the magical children's adventure, *Marlon McDoogle's Magical Night*.

Sean enjoys shooting movies, writing weirdo children's books with his weirdo friends, and speaking at universities and conferences internationally, but he hangs his nunchucks in Deadwood, SD. Inquiries at speaking@seancovel.com.

Photo by Riley Winter

ABOUT THE ILLUSTRATOR

REBECCA SWIFT should've had a perfectly reasonable career in a perfectly reasonable field. This is due to having excellent parents. Imagine their concern as their daughter expressed interest in all things "the arts."

In addition to drawing doodles and painting pictures, Rebecca is an established singer-songwriter, having been on American Idol and releasing her first album *North of Normal* later that same year. When not art-ing up the place, Rebecca works as a professional makeup artist. Which is still art. But on faces.

Rebecca is a proud mum to two girls (Quinn and Logan) and a lil dude (Tommy). The three were in no way an inspiration for the *Porter the Hoarder* series. Except that they were. Completely. Logan has a thing for stashing candy that is borderline intervention inspiring. ...It's a concern.

Rebecca hangs her many, many (many) hats in Bridgewater, SD.

Photo by Russ Hadden

If You Like This Book, ...Check These Out!

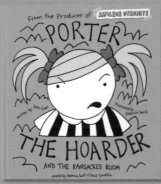
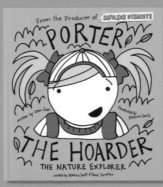
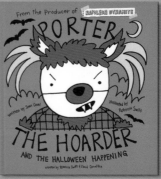